THE ULTIMATE
CHICAGO BULLS
TRIVIA BOOK

A Collection of Amazing Trivia Quizzes
and Fun Facts for Die-Hard Bulls Fans!

Ray Walker

CONTENTS

INTRODUCTION

Team fandom should be inspirational. Our attachment to our favorite teams should fill us with pride, excitement, loyalty, and a sense of fulfillment, knowing that we are part of a community with many other fans who feel the same way.

Chicago Bulls fans are no exception. With a rich, successful history in the NBA, the Bulls have inspired their supporters to strive for greatness with their tradition of colorful players, memorable eras, big moves, and unique moments.

This book is meant to be a celebration of those moments and an examination of the collection of interesting, impressive, and important details that allow us to understand the full stories behind the players and the team.

You may use the book as you wish. Each chapter contains 20 quiz questions in a mixture of multiple-choice/true or false formats, an answer key (don't worry, it's on a separate page!), and a section of ten "Did You Know" factoids about the team.

Some will use it to test themselves with the quiz questions. How much Chicago Bulls history did you really know? How many of the finer points can you remember? Some will use it competitively (isn't that the heart of sports?), waging contests with friends and fellow devotees to see who can lay claim to being the biggest fan. Some will enjoy it as a learning experience, gaining insight to enrich their fandom and add color to their understanding of their favorite team. Still others may use it to teach, sharing the wonderful anecdotes inside to inspire a new generation of fans to hop aboard the Bulls bandwagon.

Whatever your purpose may be, we hope you enjoy delving into the amazing background of Chicago Bulls basketball!

Oh… for the record, information and statistics in this book are current up to the beginning of 2020. The Bulls will surely topple more records and win more awards as the seasons pass, so keep this in mind when you're watching the next game with your friends, and someone starts a conversation with "Did you know…."

CHAPTER 1:

ORIGINS AND HISTORY

QUIZ TIME!

1. In which year did the Chicago Bulls begin playing in the National Basketball Association?

    a. 1947
    b. 1955
    c. 1966
    d. 1973

2. The franchise was nearly called the Chicago Dragons, partly to fit alphabetically behind the Bears and Cubs and party to honor a defunct rugby team from the city by that name.

    a. True
    b. False

3. Which of the following ideas did NOT play a significant role in choosing the nickname "Bulls" for the new team?

    a. The name tied into Chicago's tradition as "the meat capital of the world."

b. The name combined with the Chicago Bears to make the city "a bull *and* bear market."

c. The name symbolized power and brute strength.

d. The name has only one syllable, like other Chicago teams such as the Bears and Cubs.

4. In which season did the Bulls begin to play in their new arena (the United Center) after spending most of their history at Chicago Stadium?

    a. 1976
    b. 1985
    c. 1994
    d. 2003

5. Who was the founder of the Chicago Bulls franchise?

    a. Bill Wirtz
    b. Jerry Reinsdorf
    c. Jerry Colangelo
    d. Dick Klein

6. In which season did the Bulls earn their first-ever NBA championship by defeating the Los Angeles Lakers?

    a. 1975
    b. 1991
    c. 1993
    d. 1996

7. The longest stretch the Bulls have gone without making the playoffs is six consecutive seasons, from 1998-99 through 2003-2004.

a. True

b. False

8. How many times in their franchise history have the Bulls won a division title?

   a. 4 times
   b. 6 times
   c. 7 times
   d. 9 times

9. Which two players were the first Bulls ever to be named as Chicago's representatives in the NBA All-Star game?

   a. Guards Guy Rodgers and Jerry Sloan
   b. Center Artis Gilmore and guard Norm Van Lier
   c. Guard Michael Jordan and forward Scottie Pippen
   d. Forward Chet Walker and guard Bob Love

10. Where do the Chicago Bulls rank among NBA franchises when it comes to most Larry O'Brien Championship Trophies won?

    a. First in the league
    b. Second in the league, tied with the Lakers
    c. Third in the league, tied with the Warriors
    d. Eighth in the league, tied with the Spurs

11. How did the Bulls fare during their 50th anniversary season in the NBA?

    a. Finished at .368, did not qualify for the playoffs
    b. Finished at .602, lost in the conference finals
    c. Finished at .500, lost in the first round of the playoffs
    d. Finished at .584, lost in the conference semifinals

12. The Bulls recorded the best record in NBA history with a 72-10 mark in 1996. That stood for 20 years until the Golden State Warriors broke it by one game with a 73-9 record in 2016.

    a. True
    b. False

13. Which team did Chicago face when it played its first-ever NBA game (which resulted in a 104-97 win for the Bulls)?

    a. New York Knicks
    b. St. Louis Hawks
    c. Boston Celtics
    d. San Francisco Warriors

14. Currently, Chicago's top development team plays in the NBA G League. What is this team called?

    a. Chicago Baby Bulls
    b. Chi-Town Air
    c. Illinois Devastators
    d. Windy City Bulls

15. Which player poured in 37 points and finished as the top scorer in the first-ever NBA game that the Chicago Bulls played?

    a. Len Chappell
    b. Jerry Sloan
    c. Guy Rodgers
    d. Bob Boozer

16. As of 2020, Chicago is tied with the Detroit Pistons and Los Angeles Lakers as the NBA franchises that have sent the most players to the Summer Olympics to represent their countries.

    a. True
    b. False

17. How did Chicago fare in its first-ever NBA playoff run?

    a. Lost in the division semifinals to the St. Louis Hawks
    b. Lost in the conference semifinals to the Los Angeles Lakers
    c. Lost in the first round to the Portland Trailblazers
    d. Lost in the NBA finals to the Boston Celtics

18. Due to low attendance figures in their early years, the Bulls decided to play some "home" games from their schedule in which other city?

    a. Detroit
    b. Kansas City
    c. Philadelphia
    d. Cleveland

19. What is the name of the Chicago Bulls' longest-tenured mascot?

    a. Matt A. Dor
    b. Toro the Terror
    c. Sammy Horns
    d. Benny the Bull

20. The Bulls are the only franchise in the league to win more than one NBA title without ever losing a series in the NBA finals.

    a. True
    b. False

QUIZ ANSWERS

1. C – 1966

2. B – False

3. B – The name combined with the Chicago Bears to make the city "a bull *and* bear market."

4. C – 1994

5. D – Dick Klein

6. B – 1991

7. A – True

8. D – 9 times

9. A – Guards Guy Rodgers and Jerry Sloan

10. C – Third in the league, tied with the Warriors

11. C – Finished at .500, lost in the first round of the playoffs

12. A – True

13. B – St. Louis Hawks

14. D – Windy City Bulls

15. C – Guy Rodgers

16. B – False

17. A – Lost in the division semifinals to the St. Louis Hawks

18. B – Kansas City

19. D – Benny the Bull

20. A – True

DID YOU KNOW?

1. During their tenure in the NBA, the Bulls have been through some organizational realignment. They were originally placed in the Western Division and played there until the NBA expanded in 1980, when they moved to the Eastern Division to make room for the new Dallas Mavericks in the West.

2. Chicago has some basketball history outside of the Bulls. It is currently home to the WNBA's Chicago Sky. There were two NBA teams in Chicago before the Bulls: the Chicago Stags played from 1946 to 1950 and the Chicago Packers took the court in 1961, became the Zephyrs in 1962, and moved to Baltimore in 1963.

3. Chicago's famous Wirtz family, who owned the NHL's Chicago Blackhawks, took over from founder Dick Klein as the second owners of the Bulls. The Wirtzes were notoriously stingy, and their low budget made success challenging for the Bulls to attain.

4. While the Bulls are an anchor tenant of the United Center, it is not their home exclusively. The arena configuration shrinks, losing about 1000 seats, to house the NHL's Blackhawks, and expands by about 3000 seats when musical acts or other entertainment comes to town.

5. As a new team entering the NBA in 1966, the Bulls paid a $1.2 million franchise fee for the right to join the league.

For context, when the Toronto Raptors joined in 1993, they paid an expansion fee of $125 million.

6. During their dynasty years, the Bulls were also famous for their player introductions, featuring a darkened arena, the iconic song "Sirius" by the Alan Parsons Project, and announcer Ray Clay working the fans into a frenzy.

7. Chicago's biggest NBA rival is generally thought to be the Detroit Pistons because the two teams battled fiercely during the 1980s and '90s, struggling against each other for supremacy and championships. The Pistons have the advantage in the head-to-head rivalry, leading the all-time series 152-149, but the Bulls have won more championships with a 6-3 edge.

8. The Bulls' victory over the Utah Jazz in the 1998 NBA finals earned higher television ratings than any other finals series before or since. The deciding Game 6 also stands as the highest-rated NBA game ever, thanks mostly to the storybook ending it provided for the league's most recognizable superstar, Michael Jordan.

9. In 1979, Chicago had a chance to select superstar Magic Johnson with the first pick in the NBA draft. Unfortunately, GM Rod Thorn lost a coin toss after calling heads. Johnson went to the Los Angeles Lakers and won multiple championships, while the Bulls settled for David Greenwood with the second overall pick.

10. In the beginning, the Bulls struggled a little, posting losing records in their first four seasons. But they quickly found

success, running off five straight winning seasons after that and missing the playoffs only once in their first nine seasons despite those initial losing records.

CHAPTER 2:

JERSEYS AND NUMBERS

QUIZ TIME!

1. When they began playing in the NBA in 1966, the Bulls used what basic color scheme for their home and away uniforms?

    a. Red, white, and blue
    b. Gold and green
    c. Red, black, and white
    d. Red, orange, and yellow

2. The numbers 0 and 00 have been banned from circulation by Chicago's ownership, as they are seen to represent a losing attitude.

    a. True
    b. False

3. During which year did the Bulls wear a special Christmas jersey that featured sleeves with numbers on them?

    a. 2013
    b. 2015

c. 2017

d. 2019

4. Which unusual color have the Bulls worn occasionally to celebrate a specific holiday?

    a. Pink, to celebrate Valentine's Day

    b. Orange, to celebrate Halloween

    c. Green, to celebrate St. Patrick's Day

    d. Yellow, to celebrate Easter

5. Aside from the usual Bulls head logo, what else have the Bulls frequently sported on the front of their jerseys?

    a. A picture of the Chicago skyline, prominently featuring the Sears Tower (now the Willis Tower)

    b. A basketball with six stripes, representing the titles won during their 1990s dynasty

    c. A picture of mascot Benny the Bull dunking a basketball

    d. The word "Chicago"

6. Which two jersey numbers have proven to be most popular with Bulls through the years, having been worn by 18 players each?

    a. 6 and 11

    b. 9 and 12

    c. 1 and 20

    d. 2 and 3

7. During Latin Nights at the United Center, the Bulls have occasionally worn a jersey that reads "Los Bulls" across the chest.

a. True

b. False

8. Who is the player who wore the highest-numbered jersey in Bulls franchise history?

    a. Roger Brown

    b. Dennis Rodman

    c. Vladimir Radmanovic

    d. Drew Gooden

9. Why did star guard Michael Jordan choose to wear number 23 on his jersey when he entered the league?

    a. The numbers represented the points he loved to score (2-pointers and 3-pointers).

    b. It was his long-held goal to win a championship by the time he was 23 years old.

    c. It was half of his older brother's number, 45 (approximately).

    d. He wanted to be the opposite of Magic Johnson, who wore number 32 for the Lakers.

10. Forward Drew Gooden is the only Chicago Bull to ever wear which of the following uniform numbers?

    a. 60

    b. 70

    c. 80

    d. 90

11. Which Bulls star was idolized by Pacers forward Danny Granger—so much so that Granger chose his own number in honor of this player?

a. Forward Dennis Rodman

b. Forward Charles Oakley

c. Center Luc Longley

d. Forward Scottie Pippen

12. Star guard Michael Jordan is the only Bull ever to have worn the number 23 on his jersey and will continue to be the only one because his number is now retired.

a. True

b. False

13. Why did star rebounder Dennis Rodman choose to wear number 91 on the back of his jersey when he came to Chicago?

a. He chose the first two digits of 911 because teams would need to call for emergency help when they faced him and the rest of that talented Bulls squad.

b. He wanted to be inspired to achieve the same success as the team did in 1991, the year the Bulls won their first NBA title.

c. He described it as a ratio; of every 10 rebound opportunities that came up, he would grab 9 and lose just 1.

d. The digits added up to 10, which was the number he'd worn previously in his career, but which was unavailable in Chicago.

14. How many jersey numbers have the Chicago Bulls retired for their former players?

a. 1

b. 4

c. 6

d. 9

15. Which player competed for the Bulls for just nine seasons, which was the shortest tenure of anyone whose number has been retired by the franchise?

   a. Forward Bob Love

   b. Guard Jerry Sloan

   c. Forward Scottie Pippen

   d. Forward Dennis Rodman

16. Seven players have worn the No. 1 for Chicago and every single one of them played the point guard position while with the team.

   a. True

   b. False

17. Lucky No. 7 has been worn by 12 Bulls players over the years. Which athlete wore this number for the longest amount of time?

   a. Forward Scott May

   b. Forward Toni Kukoc

   c. Guard Justin Holiday

   d. Guard Ben Gordon

18. Who is the most recent Bulls player to have his number retired by the club?

   a. Guard Michael Jordan

   b. Forward Bob Love

   c. Forward Scottie Pippen

   d. Guard Steve Kerr

19. Which numbers did guards Jerry Sloan and Guy Rodgers, who were named the first all-stars in Bulls history, wear on the back of their jerseys in 1966-67?

    a. 1 and 2
    b. 7 and 9
    c. 4 and 5
    d. 21 and 31

20. During Ladies Nights at the United Center, the Bulls have worn jerseys that show the female form of the animal and read "Cows" across the chest.

    a. True
    b. False

QUIZ ANSWERS

1. C – Red, black, and white

2. B – False

3. A – 2013

4. C – Green, to celebrate St. Patrick's Day

5. D – The word "Chicago"

6. A – 6 and 11

7. A – True

8. B – Dennis Rodman

9. C – It was half of his older brother's number, 45 (approximately)

10. D – 90

11. D – Forward Scottie Pippen

12. B – False

13. D – The digits added up to 10, which was the number he'd worn previously in his career, but which was unavailable in Chicago.

14. B – 4

15. A – Forward Bob Love

16. B – False

17. B – Forward Toni Kukoc

18. C – Forward Scottie Pippen

19. C – 4 and 5

20. B – False

DID YOU KNOW?

1. In 2005, Chicago decided to honor the professional team that existed in the city before the Bulls came to town, the Chicago Stags. They did this by pairing their red jerseys with blue shorts that featured a Stags patch. While it was a nice idea, the clashing color combination did not earn positive reviews.

2. Star Bulls guard Michael Jordan famously wore number 23 during his first stint with the team and number 45 for a period after returning from retirement. But for one game during the 1990 season, Jordan wore number 12 for a single game after his regular jersey was stolen.

3. The Bulls have raised a banner to the rafters to honor coach Phil Jackson. Since Jackson wore no number, the banner shows his initials, P.J., instead. General manager Jerry Krause received the same treatment, and his J.K. banner also hangs in the United Center.

4. Some numbers have proven unpopular with Chicago players. Forty-seven numbers have gone unused in franchise history, as no Bull has ever worn a jersey with the following numbers: 29, 36, 37, 46, 47, 49, 56, 57, 58, 59, 60, 61, 62, 62, 64, 65, 66, 67, 68, 69, 70, 71, 71, 73, 74, 75, 76, 78, 79, 80, 81, 82, 83, 84, 85, 86, 87, 88, 89, 92, 93, 94, 95, 96, 97, 98, or 99.

5. No Chicago Bull has ever worn a jersey with a number

higher than 60 for longer than three seasons before switching numbers or leaving the team.

6. For a time in the late 1990s, the team wore uniforms with pinstripes running vertically through them. The look was popular with fans, but it was only used as an alternate.

7. Superstition may have scared some Bulls away from wearing No. 13. Only seven players in franchise history have chosen it for themselves, although Joakim Noah did have success wearing the number for nine seasons with Chicago.

8. Aside from St. Patrick's Day, the Bulls also wore green during the 2009 season to support the NBA's "Go Green" environmental initiative. It was a worthy cause, but not the team's best look.

9. Eight players have worn No. 0 for the Bulls, but only one has ever donned 00. Center Robert Parish put two zeroes on his back for Chicago during the 1997 season. Parish had worn the number since his high school days, saying that it was the only jersey left when he began playing.

10. For their Christmas game in 2014, the Bulls wore a special jersey featuring players' first names below the number on the back. Jimmy Butler's "21 Jimmy" jersey was quite popular with the fans.

CHAPTER 3:

CATCHY NICKNAMES

QUIZ TIME!

1. Which franchise nickname for the Chicago Bulls was popularized by a recurring sketch on Saturday Night Live during the early 1990s that featured Chris Farley, Mike Myers, and George Wendt as stereotypical Chicago fans?

   a. Unstoppabulls
   b. The Horns
   c. The Jordan Squad
   d. Da Bulls

2. Bulls sharpshooting guard Steve Kerr was often referred to as "The Alaskan Assassin," a combination of his birthplace and three-point shooting proficiency.

   a. True
   b. False

3. The longtime home of the Bulls, Chicago Stadium, was also more commonly known by which popular nickname?

   a. "The Bullpen"
   b. "The Wind Tunnel"

c. "The Madhouse on Madison"

d. "Hemingway's Theater"

4. Which Bulls shooting guard was known simply by the nickname "Rip"?

   a. Reggie Theus

   b. Jerry Sloan

   c. Richard Hamilton

   d. Denzel Valentine

5. Why was Chicago's small forward Bob Love nicknamed "Butterbean"?

   a. As a child, he loved eating that particular vegetable.

   b. He was lean like a string bean with moves that were smooth like butter.

   c. The Chicago offense never featured him as a "main course" but he was always a popular "side dish" option.

   d. The bean originated in Madagascar, which was also Love's birthplace.

6. Which of the following is NOT a nickname that was given to superstar Bulls guard Michael Jordan during his spectacular career?

   a. "Black Jesus"

   b. "Air Jordan"

   c. "Captain Marvel"

   d. "Jam Master Jordan"

7. After engaging in two memorable fights with his former Chicago teammates as a newly traded member of the New York Knicks, ex-Bull Charles Oakley earned the nickname "The Bullfighter."

   a. True
   b. False

8. Which single syllable does current Bull Denzel Valentine prefer to go by as his most commonly used nickname?

   a. "Den"
   b. "Zel"
   c. "Val"
   d. "Tine"

9. At times during his tenure in Chicago, Bulls forward Toni Kukoc was referred to by all of the following nicknames except for which one?

   a. "The Waiter"
   b. "Smooth T"
   c. "The Croatian Sensation"
   d. "Euro-Magic"

10. For which reasons did current Bulls swingman Zach Levine refer to teammate Coby White as "Human Flamethrower"?

   a. White's fiery temperament and willingness to express incendiary opinions
   b. White's tendency to "light up any room he enters" with his cheerful personality

c. White's ability to draw defenders to him "like moths to a flame"

d. White's shooting prowess and multiple ways to score

11. Which Bulls player was known to fans and teammates by the nickname "The A-Train"?

    a. Center Artis Gilmore

    b. Guard B.J. Armstrong

    c. Forward Ron Artest

    d. Center Antonio Davis

12. Chicago center Ben Wallace was called "Uncle Ben" by his young teammates because he was brought in to provide leadership and playoff experience while demonstrating how to act like a professional athlete.

    a. True

    b. False

13. Which current Bulls big man is known to teammates by the nickname "The Block Panther"?

    a. Daniel Gafford

    b. Luke Kornet

    c. Wendell Carter Jr.

    d. Cristiano Felicio

14. Why did teammates call Bulls forward Dennis Rodman by the nickname "The Worm"?

    a. Because he often did a dance called "the worm" during his many crazy parties.

    b. Because he wriggled like a worm when working the flippers on pinball machines.

c. Because after Rodman immediately bounced up from a hard foul in practice, a teammate remarked that "he's like a worm cut in half...he just keeps going no matter what."

d. Because he seemed to come out and play his best during the rainy season in Chicago.

15. By which short form of his name was Chicago center Robin Lopez commonly known?

a. "Rob Lo"
b. "Rolo"
c. "R-Pez"
d. "Robbie L"

16. Chicago center Robert Parish was nicknamed "The Chief" because his facial features and lack of expression were similar to a character who went by that name in the Hollywood hit movie *One Flew Over the Cuckoo's Nest*.

a. True
b. False

17. Which of the following is NOT a nickname that was given to Bulls draftee Jamal Crawford for his notable scoring capabilities?

a. "Mr. And-One"
b. "J-Crossover"
c. "Crawssover Crawford"
d. "The Ankle-Breaker"

18. Chicago swingman Jimmy Butler was such an effective scorer that he was given which of the following nicknames?

    a. "The Rainmaker"
    b. "Jimmy Buckets"
    c. "Mr. Box Score"
    d. "Jimmy 30"

19. Longtime Bulls guard Derrick Rose was given his nickname by his grandmother when he was a young child. What was the name that stuck with him all those years and into the NBA?

    a. "Rosy"
    b. "Dare Bear"
    c. "Sport"
    d. "Pooh"

20. Chicago forward Ron Artest was known as "The Shaq Stopper" because of his defensive success when guarding opposing center Shaquille O'Neal, who was notoriously difficult to play against.

    a. True
    b. False

QUIZ ANSWERS

1. D – Da Bulls
2. B – False
3. C – "The Madhouse on Madison"
4. C – Richard Hamilton
5. A – As a child, he loved eating that particular vegetable.
6. D – "Jam Master Jordan"
7. B – False
8. B – "Zel"
9. B – "Smooth T"
10. D – White's shooting prowess and multiple ways to score
11. A – Center Artis Gilmore
12. B – False
13. C – Wendell Carter Jr.
14. B – Because he wriggled like a worm when working the flippers on pinball machines.
15. B – "Rolo"
16. A – True
17. D – "The Ankle-Breaker"
18. B – "Jimmy Buckets"
19. D – "Pooh"
20. B – False

DID YOU KNOW?

1. Bulls founder Dick Klein stated that he settled on the "Bulls" nickname after mulling over ideas such as the Toreadors or Matadors. Klein voiced those ideas to his son but adopted the chosen moniker after his son told him "Dad, that's a bunch of bull!"

2. Bulls coach Phil Jackson had some quirky methods, but they were undeniably effective, as evidenced by his 11 NBA championship wins as a coach. Jackson's calm demeanor and philosophical tactics earned him the nickname "The Zen Master."

3. Chicago shooting guard Fred Hoiberg was so popular when he played college basketball in Iowa that he was nicknamed "The Mayor." Hoiberg was given the moniker after quite a few fans voted for him as a write-in candidate during the Ames, Iowa, mayoral election of 1993, and the results became a minor news story.

4. Only three athletes from Finland have played in the NBA. Current Bulls big man Lauri Markkanen is one of them. His unique nationality and consistent shooting stroke led to his frequently used nickname, "The Finnisher."

5. British Bulls guard Ben Gordon performed so well for his college team, the University of Connecticut Huskies, in important games at big venues that he earned the respectful nickname "Madison Square Gordon."

6. The current Bulls arena, the United Center, was constructed during the successful heyday of the Bulls' first dynasty (the early 1990s). The financial success brought by the team, and the marketable Michael Jordan especially, meant that when it was opened in 1994 it was often referred to as "The House that Jordan Built."

7. Dynamic duo Michael Jordan and Scottie Pippen created such an effective partnership in Chicago that they were often called "Batman" and "Robin" by media and fans. Naturally, Jordan's ultra-competitive nature meant that he was considered "Batman," while Pippen filled the sidekick role of "Robin."

8. Bulls shooting guard Brent Barry was so thin during his college career that his Oregon State teammates gave him the nickname "Bones."

9. A noted free spirit, the Bulls forward born as Ronald Williams Artest Jr. eventually decided to change his name and legally had it switched to "Metta World Peace" in 2011. In 2020, he stayed away from "Ron" and kept the "Metta" but legally changed his last name to "Sandiford-Artest."

10. Two members of the Bulls can be called "Dream Teamers" after suiting up for the 1992 United States men's Olympic basketball team. That was the first Olympics at which NBA players were permitted to participate. Both Michael Jordan and Scottie Pippen were selected to represent America and led the team to a gold medal performance.

CHAPTER 4:

ALMA MATERS

QUIZ TIME!

1. Hall of Fame forward Scottie Pippen was not as highly scouted as many other players because he attended which little known college?

    a. Cal-Poly Technical Institute
    b. Alliant International University
    c. Austin Peay State University
    d. University of Central Arkansas

2. Fan-favorite point guard B.J. Armstrong is the only player the Bulls have ever selected who played in college for the Iowa Hawkeyes.

    a. True
    b. False

3. The Bulls selected two teammates from the University of Connecticut Huskies back to back in the 2000 NBA draft. Which teammates did they choose with the 33rd and 34th picks?

a. Center Jake Voskuhl and guard Khalid El-Amin
b. Guards Ben Gordon and A.J. Guyton
c. Center Travis Knight and forward Marcus Fizer
d. Guard Michael Ruffin and forward Trenton Hassell

4. The Bulls drafted two players from the Oklahoma Sooners who would go on to play more than 400 NBA games each. Who were these players?

a. Guard Jalen Rose and center Tom Boerwinkle
b. Guard Ron Harper and center Bill Wennington
c. Centers Clifford Ray and Stacey King
d. Guards Norm Van Lier and Steve Kerr

5. Which college team did Australian center Luc Longley play for before his entrance into the NBA in 1991?

a. University of New Mexico Lobos
b. Harvard Crimson
c. University of Melbourne Boars
d. University of Sydney Dingoes

6. The Bulls hit on two top ten picks from the University of Texas but unfortunately traded both away before either ever played a game with Chicago. Which two high choices did the team miss out on?

a. Center Larry Krystkowiak and guard Gary Harris
b. Forward Maurice Lucas and guard Rodney Carney
c. Forward Norris Cole and center Matt Bonner
d. Centers Chris Mihm and LaMarcus Aldridge

7. Bulls center Tom Boerwinkle attended the University of Tennessee, where he was so popular on campus that he was known as "Tennessee Tom."

   a. True
   b. False

8. Only one Ivy League player has played for the Bulls after being drafted by them. Which player stands alone in this respect?

   a. Forward Ron Haigler from the University of Pennsylvania
   b. Guard Steve Kerr from Yale University
   c. Center Marcus Robinson from Dartmouth University
   d. Center Dave Newmark from Columbia University

9. Forward Orlando Woolridge played four years of college ball for which program before being drafted by the Chicago Bulls?

   a. Notre Dame Fighting Irish
   b. Arizona Wildcats
   c. Arkansas Razorbacks
   d. Maryland Terrapins

10. Which player, drafted by the Bulls from the UCLA Bruins, went on to have the best NBA career?

   a. Forward James Wilkes
   b. Forward Jack Haley
   c. Forward Dave Greenwood
   d. Guard Mike Lynn

11. First-ever Chicago Bulls draft choice Dave Schellhase attended Purdue University, where he played for the basketball team that went by which unusual nickname?

    a. Lumberjacks
    b. Boilermakers
    c. Golden Flashes
    d. Purple Aces

12. Michael Jordan, who was chosen 3rd overall in 1984, is the highest-drafted player the Bulls have ever selected from the University of North Carolina Tar Heels.

    a. True
    b. False

13. The high-scoring Jimmy Butler was a member of which college squad before his time on the court with the Bulls?

    a. Gonzaga Bulldogs
    b. Kansas Jayhawks
    c. UCLA Bruins
    d. Marquette Golden Eagles

14. The St. John's Red Storm provided the Bulls with which mercurial but useful player?

    a. Forward Ron Artest
    b. Forward Dennis Rodman
    c. Guard Quintin Daily
    d. Forward Scott Burrell

15. Power forward Horace Grant was drafted by the Bulls out of which school that is better known as a football powerhouse than a basketball school?

a. Alabama University

b. Clemson University

c. Louisiana State University

d. Nebraska University

16. After high-schooler Eddy Curry's career did not develop as they desired, the Chicago Bulls never again drafted another high school player.

    a. True

    b. False

17. From which of the following college basketball programs have the Chicago Bulls drafted the most players?

    a. Texas Longhorns

    b. Texas A&M Aggies

    c. Texas Tech Red Raiders

    d. Texas-El Paso Miners

18. Center Artis Gilmore played for Jacksonville University before starring with the Bulls. What was his college team's nickname?

    a. The Alligators

    b. The Dolphins

    c. The Manatees

    d. The Jacks

19. Top overall pick Derrick Rose played his college basketball as the point guard for which program before coming to the Bulls?

    a. Kentucky Wildcats

    b. Oregon Ducks

c. Memphis Tigers

d. Miami Hurricanes

20. The Bulls have drafted more players from the Michigan State Spartans than from the Michigan Wolverines.

a. True

b. False

QUIZ ANSWERS

1. D – University of Central Arkansas

2. B – False

3. A – Center Jake Voskuhl and guard Khalid El-Amin

4. C – Centers Clifford Ray and Stacey King

5. A – University of New Mexico Lobos

6. D – Centers Chris Mihm and LaMarcus Aldridge

7. B – False

8. D – Center Dave Newmark from Columbia University

9. A – Notre Dame Fighting Irish

10. C – Forward Dave Greenwood

11. B – Boilermakers

12. A – True

13. D – Marquette Golden Eagles

14. A – Forward Ron Artest

15. B – Clemson University

16. A – True

17. A – Texas Longhorns

18. B – The Dolphins

19. C – Memphis Tigers

20. A – True

DID YOU KNOW?

1. Bulls center Tyson Chandler did not attend college but rather went "prep-to-pro" and was drafted into the NBA directly out of high school by the Los Angeles Clippers, who traded him quickly to Chicago.

2. Chicago has made two University of Nevada Las Vegas Runnin' Rebels players top-10 picks in the NBA draft. The team selected guard Reggie Theus ninth overall in 1978 and forward Sidney Green fifth overall in 1983.

3. In the 1960s and 1970s, the Bulls chose four players out of West Texas A&M University. Unfortunately, Simmie Hill, Dale Blaut, Ralph Houston, and Dallas Smith all failed to crack Chicago's lineup and Chicago has not chosen another player from the school since 1976.

4. The Bulls helped make history when they drafted center Joakim Noah out of Florida with the ninth overall pick in the 2007 NBA draft. Noah's Florida teammates Al Horford and Corey Brewer had been chosen third overall and seventh overall, respectively, in the same draft. This made them the highest chosen trio of teammates in a single draft in college history.

5. The most players Chicago has drafted from any school is seven. This mark is shared by a few colleges, including Duke University, UCLA, Maryland University, and Michigan State University.

6. Chicago has selected three Duke Blue Devils within the top 10 picks of the NBA draft. They chose power forward Elton Brand first overall in 1999, point guard Jay Williams second overall in 2002, and center Wendell Carter seventh overall in 2018. Brand has a long and successful career, Williams was injured in a motorcycle accident and never recovered enough to play. The jury is still out on Carter.

7. Power forward Dennis Rodman was lucky to be noticed by NBA scouts. Rodman played first at North Central Texas Community College and then for the Southeastern Oklahoma State Savages, two schools that do not traditionally receive much attention from NBA teams.

8. During the 1979-80 season, the Bulls paired point guard Reggie Theus and shooting guard Ricky Sobers in their backcourt, creating a tandem of UNLV Runnin' Rebels.

9. Center Will Perdue remains the only Vanderbilt Commodore ever taken by the Chicago Bulls in an NBA draft.

10. 'The Bulls have drafted two players from Chicago State University: Mike Eversley in 1979 and Terry Bradley in 1983. Neither local product suited up for the team and the Bulls have yet to find a really strong local success story through the draft.

CHAPTER 5:

STATISTICALLY SPEAKING

QUIZ TIME!

1. What is the most victories recorded by the Bulls in a single regular season?

    a. 62 wins

    b. 67 wins

    c. 69 wins

    d. 72 wins

2. No one in Bulls history is within 500 assists of Michael Jordan at the top of Chicago's record book.

    a. True

    b. False

3. Six players have recorded over 5000 career rebounds for the Bulls. Which one of them has grabbed the most?

    a. Center Joakim Noah

    b. Center Artis Gilmore

    c. Guard Michael Jordan

    d. Center Tom Boerwinkle

4. Who is the Bulls' single-season leader for the most triple-doubles, with 15?

    a. Forward Jimmy Butler
    b. Guard Michael Jordan
    c. Forward Scottie Pippen
    d. Center Joakim Noah

5. This Bull really made his shots count, showing his accuracy with the highest career shooting percentage for the team.

    a. Guard Steve Kerr
    b. Center Artis Gilmore
    c. Forward Orlando Woolridge
    d. Center Eddy Curry

6. The most personal fouls most committed in any season by a Chicago player is 317. Which two aggressive players share this club record?

    a. Forward Charles Oakley and center Bill Cartwright
    b. Forward Dennis Rodman and guard Jamal Crawford
    c. Forward Dave Greenwood and center Tyson Chandler
    d. Center Tom Boerwinkle and forward Mickey Johnson

7. Shooting guard Michael Jordan has *missed* more field goals during his Bulls career than any other Chicago player has even *attempted*.

    a. True
    b. False

8. Which player holds the Chicago Bulls record for most blocks in a single season, with 220?

   a. Center Artis Gilmore
   b. Forward Nate Thurmond
   c. Center Pau Gasol
   d. Center Ben Wallace

9. Which Bull has played more NBA games with the franchise than any other player?

   a. Guard Kirk Hinrich
   b. Forward Scottie Pippen
   c. Guard John Paxson
   d. Guard Michael Jordan

10. The talented Michael Jordan is Chicago's all-time leader in points scored. How many points did he score for the team?

    a. 29,277 points
    b. 31, 380 points
    c. 38, 906 points
    d. 44, 117 points

11. Michael Jordan also holds the single-season Bulls record for points per game. How many points did he average during that 1986-87 season?

    a. 31.5 points per game
    b. 34.9 points per game
    c. 37.1 points per game
    d. 40.2 points per game

12. Michael Jordan attempted more than double the number of career free throws for the Bulls as Scottie Pippen, who is in second place on the franchise list.

    a. True
    b. False

13. Which Bulls shooter sank the highest number of free throws while playing with the club?

    a. Forward Luol Deng
    b. Guard Michael Jordan
    c. Guard Jerry Sloan
    d. Forward Bob Love

14. On the Bulls' top 10 list for points scored by a player in a season, how many times does Michael Jordan's name appear?

    a. 5
    b. 7
    c. 8
    d. 10

15. How many Bulls have had over 5000 field goal attempts for the club during their careers?

    a. 0
    b. 1
    c. 2
    d. 3

16. Chicago's Zach LaVine hit 184 three-pointers during the 2019-20 season, which set a new franchise record.

a. True

b. False

17. Which player recorded the highest career three-point shooting percentage with the Bulls, with 47.9% percent made?

a. Guard B.J. Armstrong

b. Guard Steve Kerr

c. Forward Kyle Korver

d. Guard D.J. Augustin

18. Which Bull recorded the most rebounds in one season for the team, with 1201?

a. Forward Dennis Rodman

b. Center Tom Boerwinkle

c. Center Artis Gilmore

d. Forward Charles Oakley

19. Which two teammates posted the highest combined steals total in a season for the Bulls, with 438?

a. Center Ben Wallace and guard Derrick Rose

b. Forwards Dennis Rodman and Scottie Pippen

c. Guard Michael Jordan and forward Scottie Pippen

d. Guard Norm Van Lier and center Artis Gilmore

20. Coach Phil Jackson's 1995-96 season is the benchmark in terms of winning percentage. During that year, he led the team to an 87.8 winning percentage in the regular season.

a. True

b. False

QUIZ ANSWERS

1. D – 72 wins

2. A – True

3. C – Guard Michael Jordan

4. B – Guard Michael Jordan

5. B – Center Artis Gilmore

6. D – Center Tom Boerwinkle and forward Mickey Johnson

7. B – False

8. A – Center Artis Gilmore

9. D – Guard Michael Jordan

10. A – 29,277 points

11. C – 37.1 points per game

12. A – True

13. B – Guard Michael Jordan

14. D – 10

15. C – 2

16. A – True

17. B – Guard Steve Kerr

18. A – Forward Dennis Rodman

19. C – Guard Michael Jordan and forward Scottie Pippen

20. A – True

DID YOU KNOW?

1. Five players have scored more than 10,000 points with the Bulls franchise. Guard Jerry Sloan and forwards Luol Deng and Bob Love have all surpassed that mark. Forward Scottie Pippen topped 15,000 points and, of course, guard Michael Jordan leads the way with 29,277.

2. Bulls icon Michael Jordan ranks fifth on the all-time list for most points in NBA history. Had Jordan not spent a portion of his prime in early retirement, he might have finished ahead of the four men above him on the list: Kobe Bryant, Lebron James, Karl Malone, and Kareem Abdul-Jabbar.

3. The inaugural season of the Bulls still stands as the roughest in team history. The 1966-67 squad committed 2205 personal fouls, the most aggressive version of the club to ever take the court. That club also scored the second-most points in franchise history, behind only the 1969-70 edition of the squad.

4. Center Artis Gilmore was a force in the paint for the Bulls. Gilmore blocked 1029 shots during his Chicago career to lead the franchise in that statistic.

5. Michael Jordan often scored in bunches, which was a sight to behold. Jordan recorded nine games with 55 points or more during his career. The next closest Bull is forward Chet Walker, with just one such outburst.

6. While Michael Jordan leads the Bulls in both career rebounds and defensive rebounds, he is only fourth in offensive rebounds. Joakim Noah, Horace Grant, and Scottie Pippen are all ahead of him in that category.

7. Guards Ron Mercer and Bob Love hold the top spots in the Bulls record books when it comes to minutes per game. The indefatigable Mercer averaged 40 minutes per game during his Bulls career but Love had the most impressive season, averaging 43 minutes a night in 1970-71.

8. The Bulls have followed a league-wide trend in expanding their number of three-pointers attempted in recent years. They set the team mark with 2549 in 2017-18. Before 2015, they had never even topped 1500 threes attempted.

9. The deadliest Bull on the free-throw line was guard Ricky Sobers. He was nearly a lock from the line in 1980-81, when he shot a team record .935 from the stripe. The only other Bull who shot better than 90% on free throws in a season was Ben Gordon, who shot .908 in 2007-2008.

10. In 1986-87, Michael Jordan had the green light and attempted 2279 shots, setting the Bulls record for most shots taken by one player in a single season. He scored 1098 times, which was good for a very respectable .482 shooting percentage.

CHAPTER 6:

THE TRADE MARKET

QUIZ TIME!

1. The very first single-player for single-player trade made by the Chicago Bulls occurred on November 25, 1966, when the Bulls received center George Wilson from Cincinnati. Which player did they give up in return?

    a. Guard John Barnhill
    b. Guard Jeff Mullins
    c. Guard Guy Rodgers
    d. Forward Len Chappell

2. Chicago has never in its history completed a trade with the Grizzlies franchise, either in Vancouver or Memphis.

    a. True
    b. False

3. In January 1968, the Bulls traded big man Erwin Mueller away, then re-acquired him nine months later before dealing him to a different team the following January. Which two teams did they send Mueller to?

a. Los Angeles Clippers and Boston Celtics

b. St. Louis Hawks and Detroit Pistons

c. Los Angeles Lakers and Seattle Supersonics

d. Cleveland Cavaliers and Houston Rockets

4. The Bulls and Los Angeles Clippers agreed on a deal in 2001 in which they exchanged which two big=name big men?

a. Centers Michael Olowokandi and Eddy Curry

b. Forwards Drew Gooden and Lamar Odom

c. Centers Luc Longley and Bill Wennington

d. Forward Elton Brand and center Tyson Chandler

5. Which useful Bulls player was NOT received from the Toronto Raptors in 2003 in exchange for Jalen Rose, Donyell Marshall, and Lonny Baxter?

a. Guard Chris Duhon

b. Center Antonio Davis

c. Forward Chris Jefferies

d. Forward Jerome Williams

6. In one of the Bulls' best trades, they acquired future Hall of Fame forward Scottie Pippen in exchange for center Olden Polynice. Which team regretted making that deal with Chicago?

a. Charlotte Hornets

b. Denver Nuggets

c. Seattle Supersonics

d. Miami Heat

7. Chicago has completed more trades with the Seattle Supersonics / Oklahoma City Thunder franchise than with any other NBA franchise.

   a. True
   b. False

8. The Bulls and San Antonio Spurs traded two of the top three-point threats in NBA history when Chicago sent guard Steve Kerr to San Antonio for forward Chuck "The Rifleman" Person in 1999. Between the two of them, how many 3-pointers did they finish their careers with?

   a. 1009
   b. 1355
   c. 1682
   d. 1946

9. Which of the following superstars has NOT been involved in a trade between the Chicago Bulls and Houston Rockets?

   a. Center Joakim Noah
   b. Forward Scottie Pippen
   c. Center Dikembe Mutombo
   d. Forward Carmelo Anthony

10. Who did the Chicago Bulls select with the first-round draft pick acquired by the team from the Atlanta Hawks in 1981?

    a. Forward Orlando Woolridge
    b. Center Ricky Frazier
    c. Guard Michael Jordan
    d. Forward Charles Oakley

11. Which tall center did the Bulls send to the San Antonio Spurs in 1995 to secure the services of rebounding specialist Dennis Rodman?

    a. Luc Longley
    b. Bill Wennington
    c. Bill Cartwright
    d. Will Perdue

12. Chicago has never in its history completed a trade with the Boston Celtics.

    a. True
    b. False

13. Who did the Bulls acquire from the San Francisco Warriors in the first trade in which they gave up three types of assets (a player, a draft pick, and cash)?

    a. Guard Jerry Sloan
    b. Guard Guy Rodgers
    c. Center Tom Boerwinkle
    d. Guard Norm Van Lier

14. From which team did the Bulls acquire useful center Omer Asik in a 2008 swap?

    a. Denver Nuggets
    b. Miami Heat
    c. Charlotte Hornets
    d. Portland Trail Blazers

15. On July 14, 2006, the Bulls made a swap with the New Orleans Hornets, giving up center Tyson Chandler and

receiving two players who went by initials rather than first names. Which initials did these players use?

a. D.J. and J.T.

b. P.J. and J.R.

c. B.B. and R.C.

d. R.J and J.P.

16. The Bulls made more trades with the Buffalo Braves during that team's one decade in Buffalo than they have made with the Clippers in the 40-plus years since the franchise moved to California.

a. True

b. False

17. Which player did Chicago NOT receive in return for sending former first overall pick Derrick Rose to the New York Knicks in 2016?

a. Guard Jose Calderon

b. Guard Frank Ntilikina

c. Center Robin Lopez

d. Guard Jerian Grant

18. When the Bulls needed to trade swingman Jimmy Butler away from Chicago in 2017, which franchise did they send him to in order to get the three-player return that they wanted?

a. Miami Heat

b. Philadelphia 76ers

c. Minnesota Timberwolves

d. Los Angeles Lakers

19. In 2008, the Bulls completed a large, three-team trade, acquiring Shannon Brown, Drew Gooden, Larry Hughes, and Cedric Simmons. The team sent out Joe Smith, Ben Wallace, Adrian Griffin, and a second-round draft pick. Who were the other two teams involved in the complicated deal?

    a. Indiana Pacers and Philadelphia 76ers

    b. Atlanta Hawks and Detroit Pistons

    c. Golden State Warriors and Minnesota Timberwolves

    d. Cleveland Cavaliers and Seattle Supersonics

20. Chicago has made more trades with the New Orleans Jazz than with the Utah Jazz.

    a. True

    b. False

QUIZ ANSWERS

1. D – Forward Len Chappell

2. B – False

3. C – Los Angeles Lakers and Seattle Supersonics

4. D – Forward Elton Brand and Center Tyson Chandler

5. A – Guard Chris Duhon

6. C – Seattle Supersonics

7. A – True

8. D – 1946

9. A – Center Joakim Noah

10. A – Forward Orlando Woolridge

11. D – Will Perdue

12. A – True

13. B – Guard Guy Rodgers

14. D – Portland Trail Blazers

15. B – P.J. and J.R.

16. A – True

17. B – Guard Frank Ntilikina

18. C – Minnesota Timberwolves

19. D – Cleveland Cavaliers and Seattle Supersonics

20. A – True

DID YOU KNOW?

1. Chicago has never acquired an actual player from the Miami Heat. They have made two trades with Miami, acquiring a second-round draft choice in each deal. The Bulls used only one of those selections to draft a player (Tommy Smith), as the other pick was not used by Chicago.

2. The Bulls and Detroit Pistons have had a fairly heated rivalry throughout their existence, particularly during the 1980s and 1990s. The two teams have set aside their dislike for each other to make a trade only four times in Chicago's 55-year tenure in the NBA.

3. In 2000, with the team committed to rebuilding, Chicago dealt away popular championship-era forward Toni Kukoc. This may not have been so bad for the fans, except that the return included the much-despised guard John Starks of New York Knicks fame. Starks would play just four games for the Bulls.

4. Chicago and Portland have a rich history of trades throughout the years. Significant players who moved between the two teams include guards Rick Adelman and Greg Anthony, forward Mickey Johnson, and centers LaMarcus Aldridge and Omer Asik.

5. The Bulls pulled off a nice maneuver in 1988-89. They dealt power forward Ed Nealy to the Phoenix Suns for

three-point specialist Craig Hodges and a second-round pick. Just 10 months later, they re-acquired Nealy for a conditional second-round pick that was never used, in effect getting him back for free.

6. Chicago has made trades with one franchise for so long that the franchise has gone by four different names. Over the years, the Bulls have traded with the Baltimore Bullets, Capital Bullets, Washington Bullets, and Washington Wizards

7. One of the worst trades made by the Bulls occurred in 2002 when they sent Metta World Peace, Brad Miller, Ron Mercer, and Kevin Ollie to the Indiana Pacers for Travis Best, Norm Richardson, Jalen Rose, and a second-round draft choice. Only Rose was a success with the Bulls, while Miller, Mercer, and Peace all contributed in Indiana.

8. In a deal that was very unpopular at the time, Chicago dealt the intimidating Charles Oakley to New York to add center Bill Cartwright and a draft choice that became center Will Perdue. This swap was widely credited with helping the Bulls reach their first NBA championship soon afterward.

9. Several Bulls team icons have been involved in trades with the Cincinnati Royals/Sacramento Kings franchise over the years. Some of the more important players to be swapped include guards Guy Rodgers, Norm Van Lier, and Reggie Theus, and forward Drew Gooden.

10. One of the larger and more impactful trades ever made by

the Bulls was completed on October 4, 2005, with the New York Knicks. Chicago sent Eddy Curry, Antonio Davis, and a first-round pick to New York, and received Jermaine Jackson, Mike Sweetney, Tim Thomas, two first-round picks, and two second-round picks in the blockbuster.

CHAPTER 7:

DRAFT DAY

QUIZ TIME!

1. Which prospect did the Bulls select with their first-ever draft choice in 1966?

    a. Forward Dave Schellhase

    b. Center Erwin Mueller

    c. Guard Clem Haskins

    d. Center Tom Boerwinkle

2. The Bulls have never held the first overall pick in the NBA draft in the entire history of the franchise.

    a. True

    b. False

3. How high did Chicago select power forward Jack Haley in the 1987 NBA entry draft?

    a. 1st round, 5th overall

    b. 2nd round, 43rd overall

    c. 4th round, 79th overall

    d. 7th round, 222nd overall

4. Which point guard did the Bulls select highest in the NBA entry draft, using a first overall choice to add the floor general to their team?

    a. B.J. Armstrong
    b. Ben Gordon
    c. Jay Williams
    d. Derrick Rose

5. Who was the first player ever selected by the Bulls in the NBA entry draft to be their lone selection for a single year?

    a. Guard George Maynor in 1979
    b. Center Will Perdue in 1988
    c. Forward Toni Kukoc in 1990
    d. Center Travis Knight in 1996

6. Which center/power forward, drafted by the Bulls, went on to score the most NBA points for another team after leaving Chicago?

    a. Horace Grant
    b. Orlando Woolridge
    c. LaMarcus Aldridge
    d. Maurice Lucas

7. Chicago has drafted precisely one player who has played only a single game in the NBA. That was point guard Jameson Curry from Oklahoma State in 2007.

    a. True
    b. False

8. The Bulls have looked to Europe for talent infrequently in the NBA entry draft, but they've chosen two players from one specific European nation, more than they have chosen from any other country besides America. Which nation was it?

    a. Serbia

    b. Croatia

    c. Bosnia

    d. Germany

9. Fan favorite Kirk Hinrich was selected in the first round with the seventh overall pick by the Chicago Bulls in 2003. Which position did he play?

    a. Guard

    b. Small forward

    c. Power forward

    d. Center

10. Who was the first player ever drafted by the Bulls who did not play for an American college team?

    a. Center Dragan Tarlac

    b. Forward Toni Kukoc

    c. Center Dalibar Bagoric

    d. Center Eddy Curry

11. When the American Basketball Association merged with the NBA in 1976, which player did the Chicago Bulls select from the Kentucky Colonels in the ensuing dispersal draft?

    a. Center Moses Malone

    b. Guard Bird Averitt

c. Forward Ron Thomas

d. Center Artis Gilmore

12. Three times during the 2000s, Chicago traded away all of its draft picks or selected players on draft day.

    a. True

    b. False

13. The Bulls struck out mightily in the 1997 NBA draft, selecting two players who scored a total of how many points in the NBA?

    a. 0

    b. 130

    c. 372

    d. 544

14. Of the draft spots in the top ten in the NBA draft, which spot has Chicago selected at more than any other?

    a. 2nd overall

    b. 4th overall

    c. 7th overall

    d. 10th overall

15. Superstar guard Michael Jordan was drafted by Chicago 3rd overall in the 1984 NBA entry draft. Which other Hall of Fame player was selected ahead of him?

    a. Center Sam Bowie of the Portland Trail Blazers

    b. Center Patrick Ewing of the New York Knicks

    c. Guard Clyde Drexler of the Portland Trail Blazers

    d. Center Hakeem Olajuwon of the Houston Rockets

16. Michael Jordan was such a talented athlete coming out of college that he was drafted in not one but three sports (basketball, baseball, and football).

    a. True
    b. False

17. Up to and including the 2019 NBA entry draft, how many player selections have the Chicago Bulls made in their history?

    a. 250
    b. 280
    c. 310
    d. 340

18. How many times in history has Chicago used a top 10 overall draft pick?

    a. 17
    b. 21
    c. 28
    d. 34

19. What is the lowest position in the NBA entry draft that the Bulls have selected a player who would go on to make the Naismith Memorial Basketball Hall of Fame?

    a. 1st overall
    b. 3rd overall
    c. 65th overall
    d. 103rd overall

20. There have been 26 players in the NBA who measured 7'3" or taller. The Bulls have never drafted any of them.

    a. True
    b. False

QUIZ ANSWERS

1. A – Forward Dave Schellhase

2. B – False

3. C – 4th round, 79th overall

4. D – Derrick Rose

5. C – Forward Toni Kukoc in 1990

6. C – LaMarcus Aldridge

7. A – True

8. D – Germany

9. A – Guard

10. B – Forward Toni Kukoc

11. D – Center Artis Gilmore

12. A – True

13. B – 130

14. C – 7th overall

15. D – Center Hakeem Olajuwon of the Houston Rockets

16. B – False

17. D – 340

18. C – 28

19. B – 3rd overall

20. A – True

DID YOU KNOW?

1. From 2001-02 through 2008-09, Chicago enjoyed a decade-long stretch in which they selected at least one player per year who lasted 500 games in the NBA. During those years, they hit on Eddy Curry, Trenton Hassell, Roger Mason, Kirk Hinrich, Matt Bonner, Chris Duhon, Ben Gordon, LaMarcus Aldridge, Joakim Noah, Derrick Rose, and James Johnson.

2. Despite the major draft success of Michael Jordan, the Bulls have only selected two other players from the University of North Carolina in their history. Guard Shammond Williams was immediately traded away in 1998, and guard Coby White remains with the club after his selection in 2019.

3. Of all the players drafted in Chicago history, power forward Horace Grant leads in most games played (1165) and rebounds grabbed (9443).

4. The Bulls have drafted over a dozen players from several colleges based in Chicago, including DePaul, Chicago State, Loyola Chicago, and Illinois. None has suited up for any games with the team.

5. The first Bulls draft pick who went on to play 1000 NBA games was guard Reggie Theus out of UNLV, whom Chicago took 9th overall in 1978. He played six seasons in Chicago and lasted 13 years in the league overall.

6. Chicago has held the 16th overall pick seven times, more than any other spot in the draft. Three times, they elected to trade the selection. When keeping it, their best draft picks from the spot have been forwards Metta World Peace and James Johnson.

7. The largest Chicago draft class ever was in 1968, when the team drafted 22 players. Five of those players made it to the NBA, including three with the Bulls, but only first-round center Tom Boerwinkle went on to have a sizable impact for the franchise.

8. In 2000, the Bulls had the unusual position of having three draft choices in a row. The team selected guard A.J. Guyton with the 32nd pick, followed by a pair of Connecticut Husky teammates in center Jake Voskuhl with the 33rd choice and guard Khalid El-Amin with the 34th selection. Voskuhl went on to have the best career, lasting 450 games in the NBA.

9. The Bulls favored Indiana players during the mid-1970s. In 1975, they spent their first two picks on Hoosier teammates Steve Green and John Laskowski. The following year, they added Indiana's Scott May with the second overall pick in the draft.

10. The latest pick the Bulls have made in the NBA draft was Bob Bissant from Loyola University New Orleans, whom the team chose 229th overall in 1970. Bissant never made it to the NBA. Forward Jackie Dinkins, the team's 150th overall pick from Voorhees College in 1971, was the latest pick they've made who actually played for the team.

CHAPTER 8:

THE GUARDS

QUIZ TIME!

1. Who was the regular starting point guard for Chicago during the team's challenging first season in the NBA in 1966-67?

    a. Dave Schellhase
    b. Bob Boozer
    c. Guy Rodgers
    d. Jerry Sloan

2. Bulls guard JoJo English once participated in a bench-clearing brawl against the New York Knicks, in which he and the Knicks' Derek Harper fought in the stands among spectators before being suspended afterward by the commissioner.

    a. True
    b. False

3. Which point guard has recorded the most career turnovers while with the Chicago Bulls?

a. Derrick Rose

b. Kirk Hinrich

c. Ben Gordon

d. Reggie Theus

4. The initials in popular Bulls guard B.J. Armstrong's name stand for what?

a. Brandon James

b. Benjamin Junior

c. Bryson Joshua

d. Barry Joseph

5. Which of the following 50-point facts about Chicago guard Jamal Crawford is NOT true?

a. Crawford is the only NBA player ever to score 50 points with four different franchises.

b. Crawford is in the top 10 NBA players of all time in most 50-point games.

c. Crawford's 51 points in a game is the highest ever by a player coming off the bench.

d. Crawford is the oldest NBA player ever to score 50 points in a game.

6. Which guard has played more minutes for the Bulls than anyone else?

a. Norm Van Lier

b. Jerry Sloan

c. Kirk Hinrich

d. Michael Jordan

7. It is a Bulls tradition for every point guard to lob an alley-oop pass for each teammate during the warmup before a home playoff game.

   a. True
   b. False

8. Which of the following is NOT true about quirky Bulls point guard Reggie Theus?

   a. He ran a business as a janitor before deciding to attend college.
   b. He had an active television career that including hosting talk shows, broadcasting sports, and starring on a sitcom.
   c. He was known as "Rush Street Reggie" because of the location of his home and his active presence at local establishments.
   d. He owned a prized racehorse named "No Bull" which won several races in the 1980s.

9. Which Bulls point guard holds the franchise record for most assists in a single game with 24?

   a. Kirk Hinrich
   b. Derrick Rose
   c. Norm Van Lier
   d. Guy Rodgers

10. Point guard Derrick Rose recorded his first NBA triple-double against which NBA team on January 17, 2011?

    a. New Jersey Nets
    b. Memphis Grizzlies

c. Dallas Mavericks

d. Los Angeles Clippers

11. Which of the following positions has popular Bulls guard Randy Brown NOT held with Chicago after retiring from his playing career?

a. Director of Player Development

b. Director of Amateur Scouting

c. Special Assistant to the General Manager

d. Assistant General Manager

12. During his rookie year, Chicago's Ben Gordon helped develop his own energy drink, dubbed BG7 (for his initials and number), which was created using mainly white tea.

a. True

b. False

13. Bulls mainstay John Paxson played over 600 NBA games with the club. Where does he rank in games played for Chicago?

a. First

b. Third

c. Fifth

d. Seventh

14. Three current Bulls guards have been with the team for three seasons; the longest current tenure in Chicago's backcourt. Which of the following guards does NOT share that tenure?

a. Zach Lavine

b. Kris Dunn

c. Coby White

d. Ryan Arcidiacono

15. Which Bulls guard tied an NBA record by sinking nine consecutive three-pointers on April 14, 2006, during a game against the Washington Wizards?

a. Derrick Rose

b. Chris Duhon

c. Ben Gordon

d. Kirk Hinrich

16. Former Bulls point guard Reggie Theus was the first guard in NBA history to hit a three-pointer after the institution of the three-point line was approved in 1979 following years of debate.

a. True

b. False

17. Longtime Bulls point guard Kirk Hinrich got his nickname "Captain Kirk" from a character on which popular and long-running television show?

a. The X - Files

b. Gilligan's Island

c. Saturday Night Live

d. Star Trek

18. Chicago point guard Derrick Rose owns which two medals from the time he spent leading the United States in the FIBA World Cups in 2010 and 2014?

a. Two silvers

b. One gold, one bronze

    c. Two golds

    d. One silver, one bronze

19. One former Chicago Bulls guard became a player agent and now he represents a current Chicago Bulls guard. Which two players are these?

    a. Steve Kerr is the agent for Coby White

    b. Fred Hoiberg is the agent for Shaquille Harrison

    c. Randy Brown is the agent for Ryan Arcidiacono

    d. B.J. Armstrong is the agent for Denzel Valentine

20. Bulls guard Ronnie Lester set an interesting record by recording 46 consecutive assists to the same player (teammate Michael Jordan).

    a. True

    b. False

QUIZ ANSWERS

1. C – Guy Rodgers
2. A – True
3. D – Reggie Theus
4. B – Benjamin Junior
5. B – Crawford is in the top 10 NBA players of all time in most 50-point games.
6. D – Michael Jordan
7. B – False
8. D – He owned a prized racehorse named "No Bull" which won several races in the 1980s.
9. D – Guy Rodgers
10. B – Memphis Grizzlies
11. B – Director of Amateur Scouting
12. A – True
13. C – Fifth place
14. C – Coby White
15. C – Ben Gordon
16. B – False
17. D – Star Trek
18. C – Two golds
19. D – B.J. Armstrong is the agent for Denzel Valentine
20. B – False

DID YOU KNOW?

1. Quintin Daily struggled to win over fans as a Bulls guard. He had legal troubles, drug-based suspensions, and a bit of a selfish attitude. One memorable incident that stuck with him involved some fan outrage over Daily's decision to have the team ball boy deliver him pizza, nachos, popcorn, and a drink during the third quarter of one of the team's games.

2. Bulls guard Jamal Crawford is one of just two men to win the NBA Sixth Man of the Year Award three times during his career. He was also just the second player ever to record over 10,000 career points as a reserve.

3. Chicago drafted point guards within the top 10 picks of the NBA draft in consecutive years in 2002 and 2003. They took Duke's Jay Williams second overall in 2002, but a week after Williams was injured in a motorcycle accident, they selected Kirk Hinrich of Kansas seventh overall in 2003. Hinrich would play with the team for over 10 years.

4. Chicago's Ben Gordon is the only player to ever win the NBA Sixth Man of the Year Award during his rookie season. Gordon accomplished this with his stellar play for the Bulls in the 2004-05 season.

5. Bulls guard Steve Kerr was born in Lebanon, as his father Malcolm was an academic who taught in the Middle East. Malcolm was fatally shot by a Lebanese militia during his

tenure as president of the American University of Beirut when Steve was just 18 years old.

6. Current Bulls guard Zach LaVine comes from an athletic family. His mother CJ played professional softball, and his father Paul was a linebacker in football who even made it to the NFL and played briefly with the Seattle Seahawks.

7. Only one point guard, who has played for the Bulls, has been enshrined in the Basketball Hall of Fame. This was Guy Rodgers, who starred for Chicago in their very first season before being dealt to the Cincinnati Royals. Rodgers was posthumously elected in 2014.

8. Technically, two shooting guards who have played for the Bulls have been enshrined in the Basketball Hall of Fame. One was Michael Jordan, who was elected in 2009 to the surprise of no one. Interestingly, Jerry Sloan, who had also played shooting guard for Chicago, was enshrined in the Hall of Fame that same year, but he was elected based on his coaching contributions rather than his playing career.

9. Bulls guard Steve Kerr is about as decorated as it gets when it comes to NBA championships. He not only won three consecutive titles with the Bulls from 1996 to 1998, but he also tacked on a fourth consecutive win with the San Antonio Spurs in 1999. He added a fifth title with the Spurs in 2003 and has tacked on three more championships as the coach of the Golden State Warriors in 2015, 2017, and 2018.

10. Chicago guard Jamal Crawford has made more four-point plays (hitting a three-pointer and then converting a free throw afterward) than any other player in NBA history.

CHAPTER 9:

THE G.O.A.T.

QUIZ TIME!

1. When the Associated Press ran a list of the top athletes of the 20th century in 1999, Michael Jordan finished second, behind only which man?

   a. Baseball's Babe Ruth
   b. Boxing's Muhammad Ali
   c. Football's Jim Brown
   d. Hockey's Wayne Gretzky

2. Michael Jordan was the first NBA player to ever become a billionaire, though not strictly from his playing contracts.

   a. True
   b. False

3. During his hiatus from basketball, Bulls guard Michael Jordan spent time playing which position for the Birmingham Barons and Scottsdale Scorpions baseball teams?

a. Outfield
b. Shortstop
c. Pitcher
d. Second Base

4. Aside from basketball, in which other popular sport did Michael Jordan own a franchise?

   a. Auto racing
   b. Lacrosse
   c. Soccer
   d. Football

5. When Michael Jordan posted 38 points against the Utah Jazz in Game 5 of the 1996-97 NBA Finals, the matchup quickly became known by which nickname?

   a. "The Revenge Game"
   b. "Michael's Moment"
   c. "The Flu Game"
   d. "The Turning Point"

6. What is the official name of the bronze Michael Jordan statue created by sculptors Omri Amrany and Julie Rottblatt-Amrany that stands outside the United Center in Chicago?

   a. "His Airness"
   b. "Man Takes Flight"
   c. "The Greatest"
   d. "The Spirit"

7. Bulls owner Jerry Reinsdorf once offered Michael Jordan a contract for the services of his (yet to be born) son, believing that Jordan's DNA and drive would lead to a second-generation superstar whenever Jordan decided to have children.

    a. True

    b. False

8. Which vice has Bulls guard Michael Jordan been linked to repeatedly throughout his NBA career and into his retirement?

    a. Drinking

    b. Drug use

    c. Gambling

    d. Overeating

9. When rookie Bulls shooting guard Michael Jordan was voted into the NBA All-Star Game, which other team's guard convinced the veterans on the team not to pass Jordan the ball?

    a. Clyde Drexler of the Portland Trail Blazers

    b. Magic Johnson of the Los Angeles Lakers

    c. John Starks of the New York Knicks

    d. Isiah Thomas of the Detroit Pistons

10. Which of the following was NOT a factor that prompted Bulls icon Michael Jordan to retire from basketball and pursue a baseball career instead?

    a. He wanted to achieve the dreams of his beloved father, who had recently been murdered.

b. He was exhausted from lengthy playoff runs and a stint with the "Dream Team"; the USA men's Olympic basketball squad.

c. He believed he would earn more endorsement opportunities by playing a second sport.

d. He needed a new challenge to feed his competitive nature, having already accomplished so many goals in the NBA.

11. How did superstar Los Angeles Lakers guard Magic Johnson compare himself to Michael Jordan in a famous comment?

a. "We both have great skills, but he just has so much desire."

b. "Michael Jordan couldn't carry my jockstrap."

c. "I believe that guy could beat a team of five of me."

d. "There's Michael Jordan and then there's the rest of us."

12. Michael Jordan appeared in a series of Nike commercials with film director Spike Lee, featuring the tag line "It's gotta be the shoes."

a. True

b. False

13. NBA contemporary Larry Bird thought that Michael Jordan was the best player ever. How did Bird describe Jordan after Jordan dropped a playoff record 63 points against Bird's Celtics in 1986?

a. "An unstoppable force of sheer will"

b. "God disguised as Michael Jordan"

c. "The only guy I should ever be an underdog against"

d. "Like poetry in motion on a basketball court"

14. Michael Jordan holds the record for the most times appearing on the cover of Sports Illustrated magazine. How many times did he grace the cover?

   a. 28
   b. 32
   c. 39
   d. 50

15. When Michael Jordan hit a playoff series-winning jump shot at the final buzzer that became known as "the Shot," which opposing player was unsuccessfully defending him?

   a. Byron Russell of the Utah Jazz
   b. Joe Dumars of the Detroit Pistons
   c. Nick Anderson of the Orlando Magic
   d. Craig Ehlo of the Cleveland Cavaliers

16. While negotiating his contact with Chicago, Michael Jordan insisted upon inserting a "Love of the Game" clause, which permitted him to play basketball against anyone he wanted, at any place, at any time.

   a. True
   b. False

17. When Michael Jordan returned to North Carolina to finish his schooling, in what subject did he earn his Bachelor of Arts degree in?

a. Sales and marketing

b. Accounting

c. Geography

d. Media relations

18. As a proud defender, Michael Jordan ranks third all-time in steals, behind which two NBA defensive greats?

a. Gary Payton and Elgin Baylor

b. Mark Jackson and Moses Malone

c. Vince Carter and Bruce Bowen

d. John Stockton and Jason Kidd

19. When Michael Jordan scored over 3,000 points in the 1986-87 season, he joined an exclusive club with only one other player who had achieved that landmark. Who was the other player?

a. Kareem Abdul-Jabbar

b. Wilt Chamberlain

c. Jerry West

d. Julius Erving

20. Michael Jordan's cultural impact was so widespread that, after his second retirement, the Cape Cod Baseball League retired the number 23 from circulation for all future players.

a. True

b. False

QUIZ ANSWERS

1. A – Baseball's Babe Ruth

2. A – True

3. A – Outfield

4. A – Auto racing

5. C – "The Flu Game"

6. D – "The Spirit"

7. B – False

8. C - Gambling

9. D – Isiah Thomas of the Detroit Pistons

10. C – He believed he would earn more endorsement opportunities by playing a second sport.

11. D – "There's Michael Jordan and then there's the rest of us."

12. A – True

13. B – "God disguised as Michael Jordan"

14. D – 50

15. D – Craig Ehlo of the Cleveland Cavaliers

16. A – True

17. C – Geography

18. D – John Stockton and Jason Kidd

19. B – Wilt Chamberlain

20. B – False

DID YOU KNOW?

1. Thanks to his fanatic conditioning, Michael Jordan was very durable despite being the target of many defenders every night. Over 15 NBA seasons, Jordan played a full 82-game slate in nine of them.

2. In 2016, Michael Jordan was honored at the White House when President Barack Obama presented him with the Presidential Medal of Freedom.

3. Michael Jordan has identical twin daughters, Ysabel and Victoria, who were born in 2014.

4. The iconic Michael Jordan found success at every level of play. In addition to his 6 NBA Championships, Jordan also won the NCAA Championship with the North Carolina Tar Heels, and gold medals with the United States team in the Summer Olympic Games (twice), Pan American Games, and FIBA Americas Championship.

5. Michael Jordan has long been actively involved with the Make-A-Wish Foundation. Jordan has raised over $5 million for the charity, helped make over 200 wishes come true, and has been named the Foundation's "Chief Wish Ambassador."

6. Along with author Mark Vancil, Jordan has written four books: Rare Air: Michael on Michael, I Can't Accept Not Trying: Michael Jordan on the Pursuit of Excellence, For

the Love of the Game: My Story, and Driven from Within.

7. Michael Jordan's talent was so impressive that the Detroit Pistons employed a strategy geared specifically to stop him rather than the whole Chicago team. Dubbed "The Jordan Rules," it involved physical play, along with double- and triple-teaming Jordan to prevent him from working his magic against them.

8. Michael Jordan starred in the Hollywood movie *Space Jam* alongside cartoon character Bugs Bunny (among others). The movie grossed $230 million globally.

9. During his retirement, Bulls star Michael Jordan successfully negotiated to purchase the Charlotte Bobcats franchise. Jordan became the first player to go on to be the majority owner of an NBA team. At the time, he was also the only African American owner of an NBA team.

10. Michael Jordan was peerless as an advertiser. His success, charisma, and marketability led to endorsements with such major companies as Nike, Coca-Cola, MCI, Hanes, Wheaties, McDonald's, Ball Park Franks, Gatorade, and Rayovac. His "Be Like Mike" campaign is one of the most memorable in advertising history.

CHAPTER 10:

CENTERS OF ATTENTION

QUIZ TIME!

1. Where was champion Bulls center Bill Wennington born?

    a. Chicago, Illinois

    b. Auckland, New Zealand

    c. Montreal, Canada

    d. Sydney, Australia

2. Chicago Bulls center Dave Corzine, who played seven years with the team, was born and raised in Illinois.

    a. True

    b. False

3. Only one player has spent his entire career of at least 10 years for the Bulls without ever starting a game for another NBA franchise. Which loyal center played only for Chicago?

    a. Pau Gasol

    b. Artis Gilmore

    c. Bill Wennington

    d. Tom Boerwinkle

4. Which Bulls center originally wanted to be a doctor to find a cure for AIDS and is currently a UNICEF Goodwill Ambassador?

   a. Bill Cartwright
   b. Luc Longley
   c. Joe Kleine
   d. Pau Gasol

5. Center Will Perdue was a key member of three championship teams in Chicago and also won a fourth NBA title with which other franchise?

   a. Detroit Pistons
   b. Houston Rockets
   c. San Antonio Spurs
   d. Los Angeles Lakers

6. Six big men have played over a decade in the NBA and finished their careers with more rebounds than points. Which three of these men have taken the court for the Chicago Bulls?

   a. Clifford Ray, Nate Thurmond, and Dennis Rodman
   b. Bill Cartwright, Luc Longley, and Tom Boerwinkle
   c. Artis Gilmore, Antonio Davis, and Tyson Chandler
   d. Eddy Curry, Scott Williams, and Stacey King

7. Bulls center Robin Lopez is one minute younger than his twin brother Brook, who also plays in the NBA.

   a. True
   b. False

8. Who is the only Bulls center to ever record a triple-double, consisting of point, rebounds, and blocks?

    a. Artis Gilmore
    b. Pau Gasol
    c. Ben Wallace
    d. Joakim Noah

9. Which Bulls center has a degree in fine arts, and can play nearly every woodwind instrument?

    a. Pau Gasol
    b. Nate Thurmond
    c. Bill Wennington
    d. Clifford Ray

10. Which five languages does Bulls center Pau Gasol speak fluently?

    a. English, Spanish, French, Italian, and Catalan
    b. English, Spanish, German, Italian, and Portuguese
    c. English, Spanish, Russian, Arabic, and French
    d. English, Spanish, French, German, and Russian

11. Which of the following is NOT a catchphrase used by former Bulls center and current color commentator Stacey King?

    a. "Give me the hot sauce!"
    b. "Who did it? The butler did it!"
    c. "That's big boy basketball right there; no boys allowed!"
    d. "Put the women and children to bed – it's getting scrappy out there!"

12. No Bulls center has ever led the team in points scored during a single game.

    a. True

    b. False

13. Only one Chicago Bull can claim to have been teammates with (arguably) the two best players in NBA history: Chicago's Michael Jordan and Cleveland's Lebron James. Which center played with both during his career?

    a. Joe Kleine

    b. Tyson Chandler

    c. Stacey King

    d. Scott Williams

14. Which Chicago Bulls center was the first player in NBA history to register a quadruple-double by notching 22 points, 14 rebounds, 13 assists, and 12 blocks against the Atlanta Hawks on October 18, 1974, in his very first game with Chicago?

    a. Artis Gilmore

    b. Nate Thurmond

    c. Tom Boerwinkle

    d. Dennis Awtrey

15. Which of the following facts about Bulls center Joakim Noah is NOT true?

    a. His father was a ranked tennis player and his mother competed in the Miss Universe pageant.

    b. He has citizenship in America, Sweden, and France.

c. He owns a jazz-themed nightclub in Chicago called "Noah's Ark."

d. He won back-to-back NCAA championships with the Florida Gators.

16. Star Spanish center Pau Gasol became the first player from outside the United States to win the NBA Rookie of the Year Award while playing for the Bulls in 2014.

a. True

b. False

17. Which Bulls center did color commentary for the team's radio broadcasts after retiring from his playing career?

a. Carlos Boozer

b. Tom Boerwinkle

c. Dave Corzine

d. Horace Grant

18. Where did eclectic Bulls pivot Joakim Noah propose to his girlfriend?

a. At the Burning Man Festival in Black Rock Desert, Nevada

b. At halftime of a Bulls vs. Knicks matchup while he was being honored at the United Center

c. At the bottom of a bungee jump, while the couple was dangling 200 feet in the air

d. At Wrigley Field, after Game 7 of the 2016 World Series, in which the Chicago Cubs ended their championship drought

19. Which center who spent time with Chicago won the NBA's Defensive Player of the Year award four times, was a finalist for the Basketball Hall of Fame, and is considered by many to be the best undrafted player in league history?

   a. Artis Gilmore
   b. Nate Thurmond
   c. John Salley
   d. Ben Wallace

20. Chicago pivot Eddy Curry led the NBA in field goal percentage in just his second season in the league.

   a. True
   b. False

QUIZ ANSWERS

1. C – Montreal, Canada

2. A – True

3. D – Tom Boerwinkle

4. D – Pau Gasol

5. C – San Antonio Spurs

6. A – Clifford Ray, Nate Thurmond, and Dennis Rodman

7. A – True

8. D – Joakim Noah

9. D – Clifford Ray

10. A – English, Spanish, French, Italian, and Catalan

11. D – "Put the women and children to bed – it's getting scrappy out there!"

12. B – False

13. D – Scott Williams

14. B – Nate Thurmond

15. C – He owns a jazz-themed nightclub in Chicago called "Noah's Ark."

16. B – False

17. B – Tom Boerwinkle

18. A – At the Burning Man Festival in Black Rock Desert, Nevada

19. D – Ben Wallace

20. A – True

DID YOU KNOW?

1. Bulls star Artis Gilmore married a woman named Enola Gay, who in turn was named after the first airplane ever to drop an atomic bomb.

2. Chicago center Nate Thurmond is one of only five players in NBA history to average over 15 rebounds for his career. Thurmond is joined by Jerry Lucas, Wilt Chamberlain, Bob Pettit, and Bill Russell.

3. Bulls center Carlos Boozer was a devout Christian and has a bible verse (Philippians 4:13) tattoo on his left arm.

4. Triple-doubles are rare for Bulls centers. So rare, in fact, that 35 years elapsed between the time Artis Gilmore notched one in 1977 and Joakim Noah recorded the next in 2012.

5. "The A-Train" Artis Gilmore was not just effective, but durable too. During his first stint with Chicago, Gilmore played 82 games in five out of six seasons. Gilmore also had an impressive streak of 670 consecutive games during his NBA career.

6. 7'2" center Luc Longley was the first Australian to ever play in the NBA. He won three championships with the Bulls during the 1990s.

7. One center commanded enough respect that his teammates voted to let him wear a headband on the court,

despite coach Scott Skiles' strict prohibition of the accessory. Ben Wallace was granted an exception after signing with the Bulls as a free agent in 2006.

8. Chicago big man Luc Longley once won an auction on eBay for the right to name a new species of shrimp that had been found. He chose the name "Lebbeus clarehanna" after his daughter Clare Hanna Longley.

9. Just five Turkish centers have ever played in the NBA. Omer Asik was the second ever to do so and enjoyed a lengthy career, including two stints with the Bulls.

10. During the Bulls' championship runs in the 1990s, McDonald's restaurants in and around Chicago created a sandwich called the "Beef Wennington" in honor of center Bill Wennington.

CHAPTER 11:

THE FORWARDS

QUIZ TIME!

1. Which Bulls forward, who was a teammate of Michael Jordan, shared another trait in common with Jordan, as they both played minor-league baseball?

    a. Horace Grant
    b. Charles Oakley
    c. Toni Kukoc
    d. Scott Burrell

2. Chicago forward Horace Grant famously wore goggles on the court because he was legally blind. After undergoing successful Lasik surgery to repair his eyes, Grant kept his signature eyewear "to help make it cool to wear goggles for the kids" who still needed to do so.

    a. True
    b. False

3. Which Bulls forward was also an All-American volleyball player during his time at the University of Arizona?

a. Jud Buechler

b. Rod Higgins

c. Coby Dietrick

d. Chet Walker

4. Chicago small forward Jerry Sloan was a noted collector, and at one point amassed a collection of over 70 of what item?

a. Stuffed and mounted deer heads

b. Opponents' basketball jerseys

c. Farm tractors

d. Bobble-head dolls

5. In perhaps the most memorable play of his esteemed career, Bulls forward Scottie Pippen dunked over an opponent, strode over the fallen opponent, and trash-talked a fan courtside after the play. Who were the opponent and fan, respectively?

a. Kobe Bryant and actor Jack Nicholson

b. Reggie Miller and talk show host David Letterman

c. Shaquille O'Neal and golfer Tiger Woods

d. Patrick Ewing and director Spike Lee

6. Which of the following television shows has Bulls forward Ron Artest NOT made an appearance on?

a. Celebrity Big Brother

b. Dancing with The Stars

c. Celebrity Jeopardy

d. Lip Sync Battle

7. Chicago forward Dennis Rodman counts a very unlikely person among his personal friends: North Korean Supreme Leader Kim Jong Un, whom Rodman met on a visit to the country in 2013.

   a. True
   b. False

8. Which type of business did Bulls enforcer and power forward Charles Oakley NOT invest in following his playing career?

   a. Hair and nail salons run by his sisters in Cleveland
   b. A series of carwashes, some of which also include oil changes and laundromats
   c. A blues-themed night club down the street from the United Center in Chicago
   d. A steakhouse chain with restaurants in Ohio and Florida

9. Which Bulls forward was the last to lead the team in scoring before Michael Jordan took over the team's scoring lead for most of his career?

   a. Charles Oakley
   b. David Greenwood
   c. Calvin Garrett
   d. Orlando Woolridge

10. During one famous play in the 1994 NBA Playoffs, Bulls forward Scottie Pippen refused to inbound the ball after being angered that coach Phil Jackson chose which other player to attempt a game-winning shot rather than himself?

a. Michael Jordan

b. Toni Kukoc

c. Ron Harper

d. Steve Kerr

11. Which of the following is NOT a fact about Chicago Bulls forward Dennis Rodman?

   a. He dated famous pop singer Madonna and married famous actress Carmen Electra.

   b. He wrestled as the tag team partner or famous wrestler Hulk Hogan at numerous events.

   c. He has had a song written about him called "Black, Red, Yellow" by famous grunge band Pearl Jam,

   d. He has written a film script with famous director Steven Spielberg, though the movie has not yet been made.

12. Before Karl "The Mailman" Malone missed two key free throws down the stretch in the 1996-97 NBA finals, Bulls forward Scottie Pippen got under Malone's skin by saying, "Just remember, the mailman doesn't deliver on Sundays."

   a. True

   b. False

13. Which of the following is NOT a true fact about Chicago Bulls small forward Jimmy Butler?

   a. He operated a coffee shop in the NBA Bubble during the COVID-19 pandemic.

   b. He appeared in a country music video by Luke Bryan called "Light It Up."

c. He proposed to his girlfriend while stuck on the Space Mountain ride at Walt Disney World.

d. He went on a vacation in Paris with actor Mark Wahlberg, whom he considers a friend.

14. Which Chicago forward enjoyed the city so much that he got married at the United Center nearly 20 years after his playing career ended?

a. Scott May

b. Stacey King

c. Bob Love

d. Nate Thurmond

15. Chicago forward Andres Nocioni has had his No. 13 retired by which nation's Basketball Confederation?

a. Brazil

b. Argentina

c. Italy

d. Spain

16. Bulls power forward Corie Blount appeared in a Whoopi Goldberg movie called "Eddie," which was released in 1996.

a. True

b. False

17. About which Bulls forward did an NBA general manager say "His story is one of the most remarkable I've seen in all my years of basketball. There were so many times in his life where he was set up to fail. Every time, he overcame just enormous odds."?

a. Dennis Rodman
b. Jimmy Butler
c. Horace Grant
d. Ron Artest

18. Which Chicago Bulls forward excelled at the free-throw line, finishing in the top 10 in free throw percentage during six separate NBA seasons?

   a. Tyrus Thomas
   b. Orlando Woolridge
   c. Chet Walker
   d. Taj Gibson

19. Aside from Michael Jordan, which Bulls forward has a bronze statue of himself created by the team and placed inside the United Center?

   a. Horace Grant
   b. Bob Love
   c. Scottie Pippen
   d. Orlando Woolridge

20. In 2010, Bulls small forward Ron Artest was the subject of an art exhibit in Toronto, Canada, which was called "Lovable Badass" and displayed the work of dozens of artists who had been inspired by the player.

   a. True
   b. False

QUIZ ANSWERS

1. D – Scott Burrell

2. A – True

3. A – Jud Buechler

4. C – Farm tractors

5. D – Patrick Ewing and director Spike Lee

6. C – Celebrity Jeopardy

7. A – True

8. C – A blues-themed night club down the street from the United Center in Chicago

9. D – Orlando Woolridge

10. B – Toni Kukoc

11. D – He has written a film script with famous director Steven Spielberg, though the movie has not yet been made.

12. A – True

13. C – He proposed to his girlfriend while stuck on the Space Mountain ride at Walt Disney World.

14. C – Bob Love

15. B – Argentina

16. A – True

17. B – Jimmy Butler

18. C – Chet Walker

19. C – Scottie Pippen

20. A – True

DID YOU KNOW?

1. Chicago small forward Scott May, an NCAA champion with Indiana in 1976, narrowly missed out on a major achievement when his son Scott Jr's Indiana team lost in the final game of the NCAA tournament in 2002. However, in 2005, his other son Sean May did help North Carolina bring home the title, thus making the Mays one of only four father/son combinations to play on an NCAA tournament champion team.

2. In his early years, Bulls small forward Ron Artest played basketball in some rough places. At one tournament, Artest saw another player die on the court after being stabbed through the back and heart with a dislodged table leg.

3. Bulls forward Lauri Markkanen is a rare seven-footer who can shoot from long distance. Markkanen set the NBA record as the quickest player to sink 100 three-pointers, accomplishing the feat in only 41 games at the beginning of his career.

4. Though the Chicago Bulls retired Bob Love's No. 10 after a fantastic playing career, Love struggled in retirement due to a stutter and resorted to a low-wage job as a busboy. After the restaurant owner paid for speech therapy classes, Love became a motivational speaker, wrote a book, and now works for the Bulls as Director of Community Relations.

5. Chicago forward Orlando Woolridge had great talent but terrible timing. Despite playing with Michael Jordan in Chicago, Magic Johnson with the Los Angeles Lakers, and Isiah Thomas with the Detroit Pistons, Woolridge never managed to be in the right city at the right time to win a title with any of those teams.

6. Bulls forward Dennis Rodman has written multiple books including *Bad as I Wanna Be* and *I Should Be Dead by Now*. Rodman promoted the first by wearing a wedding dress, and the second by lounging in a coffin.

7. Star Chicago forward Scottie Pippen's best season may have come without Michael Jordan in 1994-95. Pippen led the Bulls in all of the important statistical categories (points, rebounds, assists, steals, and blocks) that season. He was the only Bull ever to accomplish the feat, and one of only five players on any team to do so.

8. Bulls forward Ron Artest once released a rap album that was studded with guest stars. The album, called "My World," featured appearances by Juvenile, Capone, Big Kap, P.Diddy, Mike Jones, and Nature.

9. Although Bulls power forward Lubara Simpkins did not play much, he was a well-respected voice in the locker room. Simpkins, better known as "Dickie" used that talent after his playing career, becoming a basketball analyst, color commentator, and motivational speaker.

10. Chicago small forward Jerry Sloan starred for the team for 10 seasons and was the first Bull to have his number

retired. But ironically, when Sloan went on to become a very respected coach of the Utah Jazz for 23 years, it was the Chicago Bulls who defeated Sloan's Jazz both times he led them to an appearance in the finals.

CHAPTER 12:

COACHES, GMS, AND OWNERS

QUIZ TIME!

1. Who served as the Bulls' first general manager?

    a. Johnny Kerr

    b. Dick Klein

    c. Jerry Krause

    d. Red Auerbach

2. The tallest coach in Chicago history was their ex-center, Bill Cartwright, who was 7'1" tall.

    a. True

    b. False

3. The Bulls' first head coach, Johnny "Red" Kerr, lasted for how long in that position with the franchise?

    a. 26 games

    b. 163 games

    c. 240 games

    d. 458 games

4. The Bulls' most recent coach, Jim Boylen, rose through the coaching ranks to lead which NCAA program?

    a. Connecticut Huskies
    b. UCLA Bruins
    c. Stanford Cardinal
    d. Utah Utes

5. Who has owned the Chicago Bulls for the longest amount of time?

    a. Lamar Hunt
    b. Dick Klein
    c. Jerry Reinsdorf
    d. Arthur Wirtz

6. Of all the Chicago bench bosses who have coached over 100 NBA games with the team, which one had the lowest winning percentage at only .205?

    a. Jim Boylen
    b. Tim Floyd
    c. Bill Cartwright
    d. Kevin Loughery

7. Bulls coach Johnny Kerr was honored with Johnny Kerr Appreciation Day in Chicago on February 10, 2009. He passed away less than three weeks later.

    a. True
    b. False

8. Which Chicago general manager once took the floor as a player for the team before getting the chance to guide it from the front office?

a. Gar Forman

b. Rod Thorn

c. John Paxson

d. Dick Motta

9. Which coach led the Bulls to their first NBA championship?

a. Phil Jackson

b. Jerry Sloan

c. Dick Motta

d. Johnny Kerr

10. How many of the Bulls 23 head coaches have spent their entire NBA coaching career with Chicago?

a. 1

b. 6

c. 11

d. 14

11. Who is the Chicago leader in all-time coaching wins with the franchise?

a. Doug Collins

b. Tom Thibodeau

c. Fred Hoiberg

d. Phil Jackson

12. Chicago is the only NBA franchise to have a player rise from playing for the team to ownership of the team.

a. True

b. False

13. Which Bulls coach played baseball for Chicago White Sox

farm teams in his youth before becoming a basketball coach?

a. Kevin Loughery
b. Fred Hoiberg
c. Vinny Del Negro
d. Scotty Robertson

14. One Chicago coach also spent part of his career in broadcasting, winning the Curt Gowdy Media Award for his efforts. Who was this coach?

a. Doug Collins
b. Phil Jackson
c. Stan Albeck
d. Scott Skiles

15. Which Bulls general manager has led the franchise to the most playoff appearances?

a. Pat Williams
b. Gar Forman
c. Jerry Krause
d. Dick Motta

16. Bulls owner Jerry Reinsdorf once proposed trading franchises with New York Yankees owner George Steinbrenner as part of a business deal.

a. True
b. False

17. Out of eight seasons coaching the Bulls, how many times did coach Dick Motta finish above .500?

a. 2

b. 4

c. 5

d. 8

18. How did Jerry Reinsdorf become the majority owner of the Chicago Bulls in 1985?

    a. He purchased the team when the previous owners wished to sell.

    b. He inherited the team from his father.

    c. He forced a takeover of the corporation that had previously owned the team.

    d. He was hired as CEO of the company that owned the team.

19. Which Bulls coach is the only one of the following NOT to have won the NBA Coach of the Year Award while behind the bench for Chicago?

    a. Tom Thibodeau

    b. Phil Jackson

    c. Johnny Kerr

    d. Scott Skiles

20. Coach Scott Skiles was not easy on players who he perceived to be lacking effort on the court. He once replied to a question about how Bulls center Eddy Curry could rebound more effectively by uttering a single word: "Jump."

    a. True

    b. False

QUIZ ANSWERS

1. B – Dick Klein

2. A – True

3. B – 163 games

4. D – Utah Utes

5. C – Jerry Reinsdorf

6. B – Tim Floyd

7. A – True

8. C – John Paxson

9. A – Phil Jackson

10. B – 6

11. D – Phil Jackson

12. B – False

13. D – Scotty Robertson

14. A – Doug Collins

15. C – Jerry Krause

16. B – False

17. C – 5

18. A – He purchased the team when the previous owners wished to sell.

19. D – Scott Skiles

20. A – True

DID YOU KNOW?

1. Johnny "Red" Kerr accomplished a few notable achievements in his first year coaching the Bulls. Although he finished with a losing record, the team became the first expansion team ever to qualify for the playoffs in its opening season. Kerr was awarded the NBA Coach of the Year Award, which is still the only time it has been given to a coach with a losing record.

2. Vinny Del Negro coached the Chicago Bulls for two seasons. In both of those seasons, he finished 41-41, for a dead-even .500 record of 82-82. This was not good enough for the Bulls, who let him go to hire Tom Thibodeau.

3. As a child, future Bulls coach Doug Collins grew up next door to famous Hollywood actor John Malkovich.

4. Only one top executive for the Chicago Bulls was born outside of the United States. That was current top man Arturas Karnisovas, the team's Executive Vice President of Basketball Operations, who was born in Lithuania.

5. Chicago coach Scott Skiles remains in the NBA record books as a player for recording the most assists ever in a single game. Skiles dished out 30 assists as a member of the Orlando Magic during the 1990-91 season.

6. Two men have served as both coach and general manager of the Chicago Bulls. Dick Motta coached the team for

eight years and handled the personnel duties for three years during that tenure. Rod Thorn spent eight years as Chicago's general manager and stepped in as coach for a brief period during one season.

7. Doug Collins coached the Chicago Bulls during the early years of Michael Jordan's career, before being let go in 1989. Nearly three decades later, he was re-hired by the team in 2017 to serve as Senior Advisor of Basketball Operations.

8. Scott Skiles preached a focus on defense during his time behind the Chicago bench and it paid off. During his tenure, the team set a franchise record by holding opponents under 100 points for 26 consecutive games.

9. Twice in league history, Chicago general managers have been awarded the NBA Executive of the Year Award. Jerry Krause received the honor in 1995-96, and Gar Forman shared the award with Miami's Pat Riley in 2010-11.

10. Chicago coach Larry Costello was an NBA point guard before stepping behind the bench. Before retiring from the Philadelphia 76ers in 1968, he was the last player in the league to use a two-handed set shot.

CHAPTER 13:

THE AWARDS SECTION

QUIZ TIME!

1. Which Bull has won the most Maurice Podoloff Trophies as league MVP?

    a. Scottie Pippen
    b. Derrick Rose
    c. Artis Gilmore
    d. Michael Jordan

2. The first Bull to win any major award given out by the NBA was franchise guard Michael Jordan.

    a. True
    b. False

3. Michael Jordan won six NBA titles while with the Bulls. How many times did he take home the NBA Finals MVP Trophy?

    a. 2
    b. 3
    c. 4
    d. 6

4. In 1996, the NBA announced its 50 Greatest Players in NBA history. How many of these players suited up for the Bulls?

   a. 1
   b. 4
   c. 5
   d. 7

5. The J. Walter Kennedy Trophy, given to an NBA player who shows "great service and dedication to the community," has been awarded to which Bull?

   a. Jay Williams
   b. Jimmy Butler
   c. Reggie Theus
   d. Joakim Noah

6. How many Bulls have won the Twyman-Stokes Trophy as NBA Teammate of the Year for "selfless play and commitment and dedication to his team"?

   a. 0
   b. 2
   c. 3
   d. 6

7. Following his second retirement, the NBA began handing out the Michael Jordan Man of Year Award to a deserving recipient from any franchise who "helped grow the game beyond his home city."

   a. True
   b. False

8. Who was the most recent Chicago player to make the NBA All-Rookie first team?

   a. Coby White in 2020
   b. Lauri Markkanen in 2018
   c. Nikola Mirotic in 2015
   d. Tyrus Thomas in 2007

9. Which Bulls player is the only one to have taken home the NBA All-Star Game MVP Award?

   a. Horace Grant
   b. Richard Hamilton
   c. Tom Boerwinkle
   d. Michael Jordan

10. Which of these Chicago icons is the only one to finish a season as the league's leader in points per game?

   a. Artis Gilmore
   b. Michael Jordan
   c. Derrick Rose
   d. Jamal Crawford

11. The Sixth Man of the Year Award for best performing player as a substitute has been won by which two Bulls in franchise history?

   a. Dennis Rodman and Luol Deng
   b. Toni Kukoc and Ben Gordon
   c. Norm Van Lier and B.J. Armstrong
   d. Dennis Rodman and B.J. Armstrong

12. In 1988, Bulls guard Michael Jordan defeated Philadelphia 76ers forward Charles Barkley in one of the most memorable NBA All-Star Weekend Slam Dunk contests of all time.

    a. True

    b. False

13. Which of the following Bulls players did NOT win the Eddie Gottlieb Trophy as the league's top rookie?

    a. Michael Jordan

    b. Toni Kukoc

    c. Elton Brand

    d. Derrick Rose

14. Of the Bulls in the Basketball Hall of Fame, Jerry Sloan was the first to play with Chicago. What year did he begin playing with the team?

    a. 1966

    b. 1968

    c. 1970

    d. 1973

15. Which Bulls player has been selected to the most NBA All-Star Games?

    a. Scottie Pippen

    b. Michael Jordan

    c. Luol Deng

    d. Steve Kerr

16. Guard Derrick Rose is the youngest Bull to ever win both the NBA Rookie of the Year Award and the NBA Most Valuable Player Award.

    a. True
    b. False

17. The Bulls have fared well at the NBA All-Star Weekend Three-Point Shootout, with six players entering and a Bull winning the event four times. Which of the following players took home this title more than once?

    a. B.J. Armstrong
    b. Craig Hodges
    c. Michael Jordan
    d. Steve Kerr

18. Who was the most recent Chicago player to make the NBA All-Defensive team?

    a. Michael Jordan
    b. Scottie Pippen
    c. Dennis Rodman
    d. Joakim Noah

19. In which years did Chicago host the NBA's annual All-Star Game?

    a. 1973, 1988, and 2020
    b. 1972 and 1995
    c. 1983, 1998, and 2017
    d. They have never hosted the All-Star Game

20. For almost two decades, IBM gave an award to the NBA player judged by its programming formulas to be most valuable to his team. Michael Jordan received the award twice for Chicago.

    a. True
    b. False

QUIZ ANSWERS

1. D – Michael Jordan

2. A – True

3. D –6

4. C – 5

5. D – Joakim Noah

6. A – 0

7. B – False

8. B – Lauri Markkanen in 2018

9. D – Michael Jordan

10. B – Michael Jordan

11. B – Toni Kukoc and Ben Gordon

12. B – False

13. B – Toni Kukoc

14. A – 1966

15. B – Michael Jordan

16. A – True

17. B – Craig Hodges

18. D – Joakim Noah

19. A – 1973, 1988, and 2020

20. A – True

DID YOU KNOW?

1. The Joe Dumars Trophy for sportsmanship, ethical behavior, fair play, and integrity has been won by only one player born outside the United States: Chicago Bulls forward Luol Deng in 2006-07. Deng was born in the United Kingdom and remains the only Bull to win this award.

2. Each year, the NBA denotes three teams' worth of All-NBA players and the Bulls have been well represented. Michael Jordan landed on the first team 10 times, while Derrick Rose and Joakim Noah each made it once. Bob Love, Norm Van Lier, and Pau Gasol have all been named to the second team. Jimmy Butler earned third-team honors. Scottie Pippen is the only Bull to appear on each of the teams; three times on the first team, twice on the second, and twice on the third.

3. Only four players have earned the NBA's relatively new Lifetime Achievement Award. No Chicago Bull has been honored with this award to date, though Michael Jordan seemingly has a strong chance to earn it in the future.

4. When the NBA announced its top 10 teams in history in 1996, Chicago was well represented. They secured two of the spots on the list, placing both the 1991-92 and the 1995-96 editions. Michael Jordan and Scottie Pippen appeared on both of those teams and Phil Jackson coached them both years.

5. Both Ben Wallace and Dennis Rodman have won multiple NBA Defensive Player of the Year Awards (they share six). But all of those were won while playing for the Detroit Pistons rather than during their tenure in Chicago.

6. Michael Jordan and Joakim Noah are the two Bulls who have won NBA Defensive Player of the Year Awards. Each took home the award once, Jordan in 1987-88 and Noah in 2013-14.

7. There is no award for one dubious record held by the Bulls; the fewest points scored in a game since their entrance to the league in 1966. Chicago netted only 49 on April 10, 1999. They also set a record that season for the lowest points per game average, with just 81.9.

8. Chicago forward Jimmy Butler turned in such a good 2015 season that he was awarded the NBA's Most Improved Player Award. He is the only Bull to receive this honor.

9. The Bulls have featured four winners of the NBA All-Star Weekend Slam Dunk Contest. Both Orlando Woolridge and Michael Jordan won the event multiple times (including back-to-back titles for each), and Scottie Pippen and Tyrus Thomas have also been declared champions.

10. Chicago's Craig Hodges remains the league record-holder at the NBA All-Star Weekend Three-Point Shootout. Hodges nailed 21 threes in one round in 1991, including 19 in a row, marksmanship marks that have yet to be broken.

CONCLUSION

There you have it, an amazing collection of Bulls trivia, information, and statistics at your fingertips! Regardless of how you fared on the quizzes, we hope that you found this book entertaining, enlightening, and educational.

Ideally, you knew many of these details, but also learned a good deal more about the history of the Chicago Bulls, their players, coaches, management, and some of the quirky stories surrounding the team. If you got a little peek into the colorful details that make being a fan so much more enjoyable, then mission accomplished!

The good news is that the trivia doesn't have to stop there! Spread the word. Challenge your fellow Bulls fans to see if they can do any better. Share some of the stories with the next generation to help them become Chicago supporters, too.

If you are a big enough Bulls fan, consider creating your own quiz with some of the details you know that weren't presented here and then test your friends to see if they can match your knowledge.

The Chicago Bulls are a storied franchise, they have a long history, with multiple periods of success and a few that were less than successful. They've had glorious superstars, iconic moments, hilarious tales, but most of all they have wonderful, passionate fans. Thank you for being one of them.

Made in the USA
Las Vegas, NV
11 November 2022